P9-DEH-214

Prices

Adult . . . .

Child . . . .

Senior . . . .

Arctic air mass settles over city.

Frigid temps will remain.

More weather after the news . . .

For Sam, Ben, Laura and Jeff—can you believe it?
— BC

To Tom, Vicky and Victor. Dare to dream.
— RH

Text © 2003 by Barbara Crispin
Illustrations © 2003 by Roswitha Houghton
All rights reserved.

Published by Dancing Words Press, Inc.
P.O. Box 1575
Severna Park, MD 21146
Visit us at www.dancingwordspress.com

Library of Congress Cataloging-in-Publication Data

Crispin, Barbara J..
    City Zoo Blizzard Revue / by Barbara Crispin ;
illustrated by Roswitha Houghton. —1st ed.
      p.   cm.
    SUMMARY: The City Zoo might close. The bitter winter
has kept visitors away. Will a show starring arctic animals in
surprising acts save the zoo?
    LCCN 2002093267
    ISBN 0-9716346-1-0
    1. Zoo animals—Juvenile fiction.   2. Zoos—Juvenile
fiction.   3. Winter—Juvenile fiction.   [1. Zoo animals—
Fiction.   2. Zoos—Fiction.   3. Winter—Fiction.]
    I. Houghton, Roswitha.   II. Title.

PZ7.C869357Ci   2003   [E]
                               QBI33-922

Production Assistance: Susan H. Hartman

Printed in USA
Berryville Graphics

First Edition

1 3 5 7 9 10 8 6 4 2

City Zoo Blizzard Revue

By Barbara Crispin
Illustrated by Roswitha Houghton

Hard times!
Rusty Sparrow stopped
snacking on birdseed.
She knew something about
hard times because she spent
each winter searching for food.
But close the zoo?
She flew off to
share the news
with her flock.

Lions →
← Zebras
Birds ↑

The flock listened to Rusty's news.
Then they scattered to spread the
word of the zoo's troubles.

The lions lazed in their rocky den.
"Who cares? It's cold. If we get hungry we can hunt for food."

The chimpanzees could hardly listen
for all their shivering and chattering.

The black bears and the
grizzlies didn't even
answer the call.
They were hibernating
until spring.

But not all of the animals minded the cold.
The penguins played tag on their frozen pond.

Percy Polar Bear paced the path
around his home. Back and forth.
His nose lifted to catch the slightest
scent of new snow. Oh, how he
loved the zoo when it snowed.

The reindeer herd roamed their
wide pen grazing and gossiping.

"Did you hear?
The birds in the
Tropical House are
staging a sit-in.

They've migrated to
the southern end of
the aviary and won't
come back until they
get more heat!"

"I heard the gazelles are sick.
The zebras' stripes are waving up
and down with their shivering
and it's giving the gazelles
motion sickness."

"Take my advice. Don't wander
too far to the end of the pen.
Tigress is restless. She shouldn't be taunted, you know."

Rusty Sparrow broke into their conversation.

"Big news! Listen up! Hard times are coming. The zoo's in trouble."

All of the reindeer started talking at once.

Rusty flew off to the next pen.

Jocko Seal was a retired circus performer.
"We need to put on a show," he said.
"People love to see a show.
Get everyone together
who doesn't mind the cold.
We've got work to do!"

Jocko searched his room.
"Where is my old circus trunk?
We can use my props."

The arctic animals came. There was Percy Polar Bear, Winston Walrus, Vixey Arctic Fox, all of the penguins and the herd of reindeer. Others showed up to help: Merton Moose, an alpaca quartet and a bighorn sheep trio named Jed, Elmer and Chauncy.

Jocko looked them over. "Let's see what we can do."

Some sang. Some danced. Some had surprising talents. Jocko could see it was going to be quite a show.

Jocko didn't wait for the others to start practicing.
1 . . . 2 . . . 3 . . . 4 . . . 5 . . . 6 snowballs whirled above him.
He loved the thrill of showtime.

Winston Walrus
started the show.
"Arugh! Arugh! Arugh!"

The zookeepers came running
to see what caused the commotion.
Pulling on hats and gloves, they rushed to the
walrus tank. They watched in surprise as the
penguins in the next tank began skating.

The line of penguins split into two, and then four.
They danced across the ice.
The zookeepers clapped.
The penguins twirled and spun,
ever graceful and smooth.
The zookeepers were amazed.

Winston wobbled over
and everyone followed.
Jocko and the seals juggled
snowballs and long pointy icicles.
They spun plates of ice on their noses
and tumbled over one another
like acrobats.

The zookeepers
clapped and cheered
for the seals.

One zookeeper
called out,
"This is great!
I'm going to get
the boss."
He ran to the
main office.

The rest of the audience moved along to the reindeer meadow where horn music could be heard.

The reindeer were huddled together in a tight circle.
Jed, Elmer and Chauncy played jazz on curled horns.
The reindeer fanned out to form a single line
and stepped in time to the music.
What rhythm! What moves!
They were stupendous!

The boss ran down in time to see their big finale—the kick line. "Bravo! Bravo!" He cheered and clapped with everyone else.

The trio's music changed tempo
and Merton shuffled out from
the bushes doing his soft shoe
routine. Tappa-tappa-tap-tap.
The reindeer watched in wonder.
One reindeer whispered,
"He's never looked so dashing."

As Merton shuffled off, the alpacas moved up to the fence.
The audience was curious and leaned closer.
"Hmmmmmm." A note was given and the humming began.
The Alpacas of the Andes barbershop quartet delighted the
audience with its folk songs from home and its moving harmonies.

The boss whispered,
"I wish I knew the words."
Then he slapped his forehead
and shouted, "Someone call
the reporters! These animals
just might save the zoo!"

The TV reporters and camera
crews rushed to the zoo

just as the Sparrow Divebombers
appeared flying in death-defying formations.

Percy and Vixey went into their act.
Vixey brought out a box and
showed the audience it was empty.
Percy put his paw through the box.
It was indeed empty.
Vixey closed the box and
balanced it on her head.
Percy tapped the box three
times with his long, sharp
claw. He opened the box
and a pigeon popped out
cooing as it flew away.
Everyone applauded.
Percy and Vixey bowed
and went on to
their next trick.
Disappearing fish.

Everything went along as Jocko predicted.
The reporters showed the animals doing
their acts on the evening news.

Now the people came to the zoo in flocks and were
herded through the acts twice a day.
The performing and the cheering and the
applauding went on like that until March when
warm weather returned and the ice thinned out.

The show was over.

Then something happened that Jocko didn't predict.
The zoo was so successful that the boss built a blizzard room.

They were cold and comfortable all summer long.